Moonlight Kite

by Helen E. Buckley
illustrated by Elise Primavera

Lothrop, Lee & Shepard Books
New York

Once there were three monks who lived in an old monastery overlooking the sea. The monastery was so old that most of the monks who had lived there were now gone, and only Brother André, Brother Blaise, and Brother Carlos were left to care for it.

Brother André worked in the garden inside the high brick wall, taking care of the vegetables and milking the goats. But when the gulls came flying in from the sea, he always stopped to watch them.

Brother Blaise worked in the kitchen. He baked bread and made big pots of stew. He always made too much, and the cat had many leftovers.

Brother Carlos was content as long as he had cloth or leather or wood in his hands. He spent his days at one of the tower windows, mending robes and sandals or fashioning small figures with his carving tools.

The monastery was a quiet place. It was especially quiet because Brother André, Brother Blaise, and Brother Carlos had taken a vow of silence in order to give more thought to their prayers. But they missed the old days, when other monks worked along with them in the fields and kitchens and workrooms, and kneeled beside them in chapel. They missed the villagers who used to come with their children to buy bread and goats' milk. And they missed the laughter of the children most of all.

Then one spring afternoon, a brother and sister—Nicholas and Anarilla—climbed the hill to the monastery. Between them they carried a large orange kite, its long tail trailing in the grass behind them. When they reached the arched doorway in the high brick wall, they stopped to rest and to unwind the kite's long string.

"Are you sure no monks live here anymore?" Anarilla asked.

"Yes," said Nicholas. "Papa says that no one has seen any monks here for a long time. Besides, this is the best hill in our village for flying kites."

"Well, if there *are* monks, I hope they don't mind *us* being here," said Anarilla, trying hard not to look at the empty monastery windows.

All afternoon, Nicholas and Anarilla flew their orange kite—sometimes together, sometimes taking turns. But when it was time to go home, they brought the kite down too quickly and it was caught in the branches of a tall tree near the monastery wall.

"Oh dear!" said Anarilla. "Now what shall we do?"

"Leave it," said Nicholas. "We'll think of a way to bring it down tomorrow." And he and Anarilla started down the hill to the village. They did not notice the faces of Brother André, Brother Blaise, and Brother Carlos in the tower window.

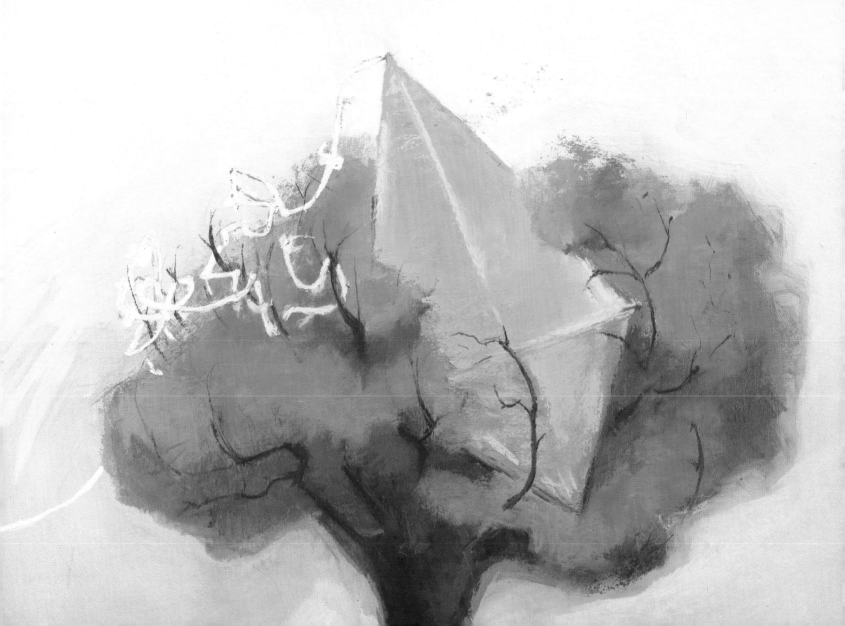

That night the three monks lay on their cots and thought
about kites. They saw them dancing far above their heads. They
remembered the push of the wind and the pull of the string. And
at almost the same moment, each of them got up from his cot, lit
his candle, and made his way along the narrow passages and
winding stone steps to the courtyard.

Light from a full moon filtered through the windows and broken places in the wall and made a wide path as the monks passed under the archway and out to the tree. And when they looked up through the branches, the orange kite seemed to be touched with gold.

Without a word, Brother André crouched by the brick wall so that Brother Blaise could climb on his back. Brother Carlos, tucking the hem of his robe into the cord around his waist, climbed first on Brother André, then on Brother Blaise, and finally lifted himself to the top of the wall. Now close to the orange kite, he reached up and brought it down.

Then Brother André held the string, and Brother Blaise and Brother Carlos held the kite, and they caught the wind and sent it flying. At first it wavered and wobbled; but when Brother André gave the line a sharp tug, the orange kite righted itself and began to climb. The moon lit up the sky, and the monks, taking turns, were once more the small boys they used to be.

For Brother André, the grass on the hill became a sandy shore, and he was running by the sea with only the gulls to keep him company.

For Brother Blaise, the hill became a flat rooftop, and he was flying the orange kite far above a crowded city street. He could hear the barking dogs and the shouting children far below him.

For Brother Carlos, the hill was a sunbaked courtyard, and the kite was flying high above the red-tiled roof of his parents' home. He could see water splashing from the fountain and smell the flowers in their earthen pots.

Far into the night, the monks flew the orange kite, watching it soar and sail, twist and turn, its long tail keeping it in perfect balance.

And when at last they were tired, they pulled the kite down
and put it in another, smaller tree. Then they went back across
the courtyard and up the winding stone steps to bed.

The next afternoon when Nicholas and Anarilla climbed the hill, they were surprised to find the kite in another tree.

"Look!" Anarilla whispered. "Maybe there *are* monks living here!"

"Pooh!" said Nicholas as he took the kite down. "The wind blew the kite from one tree to another."

But Anarilla could not help looking up at the monastery window. "I *know* the monks are there," she said.

"Don't be a goose," said Nicholas. But he, too, looked up at the monastery as if he expected to see someone.

Then he and Anarilla began to fly the kite, and they soon forgot the monks.

Still, when it was time to go home, Anarilla said, "Let's leave the kite in the tree again. Maybe monks like to fly kites too!"

"That's silly," said Nicholas, "but I guess it *will* be easier than carrying it."

As the monks watched the children go down the hill, they turned to one another as if to say, "They have left the kite, and the moon will be bright again tonight!" Then Brother Carlos hurried over to his workbench. He had an idea.

The next afternoon, Nicholas and Anarilla climbed the hill again. Suddenly they stopped and stared. In the small tree, a blue kite hung next to the orange one.

"I told you so, Nicholas!" Anarilla cried. "There *are* monks living here. They have made a kite for us."

Nicholas looked first at the blue kite and then up at the monastery. For just a moment, he thought he saw something move behind the tower window. "You're right, Anarilla," he said softly. Then he took down the blue kite and handed it to her.

So it came about that when the wind was right, Nicholas and Anarilla flew the kites by day, and the monks flew them by night. Soon more children came with kites, and the sky was filled with their colors. And when the children's shouts and laughter reached the monastery, the monks stopped for a moment and smiled before going on with their work.

And often on a summer evening, just before going to bed,
Nicholas and Anarilla looked up the hill toward the monastery, and
saw the shadowy figures of Brother André, Brother Blaise, and
Brother Carlos flying kites in the moonlight.

Ƒor Georgia and Nancy Zughaib
with whom it all began
—HEB

Lothrop, Lee & Shepard Books, a division of William Morrow & Company, Inc.,
1350 Avenue of the Americas, New York, New York 10019.
Printed in Singapore
First Edition   2 3 4 5 6 7 8 9 10
Library of Congress Cataloging in Publication Data. Buckley, Helen Elizabeth.
Moonlight Kite / by Helen E. Buckley; illustrated by Elise Primavera.
p.   cm. Summary: The last three monks at a monastery have their lives enriched by
the presence of children flying kites outside their walls.
ISBN 0-688-10931-4. — ISBN 0-688-10932-2 (lib. bdg.)
[1. Kites—Fiction. 2. Monasteries—Fiction. 3. Religious life—Fiction.]
I. Primavera, Elise, ill. II. Title. PZ7.B8820Mo 1995 [E]—dc20 91-34285 CIP AC

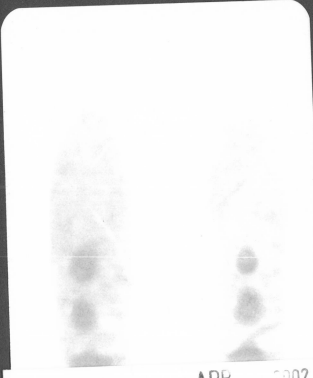